Split! Splat!

BY **AMY GIBSON**

ILLUSTRATED BY **STEVE BJÖRKMAN**

SCHOLASTIC PRESS · NEW YORK

LIBRARY OF CONGRESS CATALOGING-IN-PUBLICATION DATA

Gibson, Amy (Amy S.)

Split! Splat! / by Amy Gibson ; [pictures by Steve Björkman] — 1st ed.   p.   cm.

Summary: When a little girl ventures out into a spring rain with her dog, singing a simple,

plain, pitter-patter rain song, her neighbors soon join her for some muddy-day fun.

[1. Stories in rhyme. 2. Rain and rainfall — Fiction. 3. Neighbors — Fiction. 4. Dogs — Fiction.]

I. Björkman, Steve, ill. II. Title.   PZ8.3.G3577Spl 2012   [E] — dc22   2011003772

ISBN 978-0-439-58753-2

10 9 8 7 6 5 4 3 2   12 13 14 15 16

Printed in Singapore   46

First edition, March 2012

The text was set in MrsEaves. The display type was set in P22Garamouche.

Book design by Marijka Kostiw

For my sister, Beth,

who believed — AG

For my adventurous daughter,

Kristi, who finds joy in exploring

all kinds of weather — SB

I sing a little rain song,

a simple song,

a plain song,

a pitter-patter-tip-tap-
on-the-windowpane song.

Pip

pip

pip

pip,

drippy drop drop drip.

Tip
    tap,
pit
    pat,
pitter patter split splat!

Splishy sploshy wishy washy —

drip

drip

drop!

I sing a little mud song,
a puddle song,
a muddle song,

a no-shoes, toes-ooze,
slip-slap-and-thud song.

Splish
sploosh,
squash
squoosh,

oochy sploochy woochy woosh!

Slip

slop,

ker-plop!

Mucka mucka chucka wucka —

splish

splash

sploosh!

I sing a little sun song,
a fun song,
a run song,

a clouds-gone,
green-lawn,
raining-is-all-done song.

Swish

swish

swish

swish,

swishy swash wish wash.

Tickle wiggle wriggle giggle,

hop

skip,

back flip —

jump thump rump

BUMP —

skip

flip

flop!

I sing a little rain song,
a mud song,
a sun song,

a clouds-cry,
mud-pie,
blue-sky
song.